LA PEQUEÑA MARIPOSA QUE SÍ PUDO

¿Dónde están las flores?

Ross Burach

Scholastic Inc.

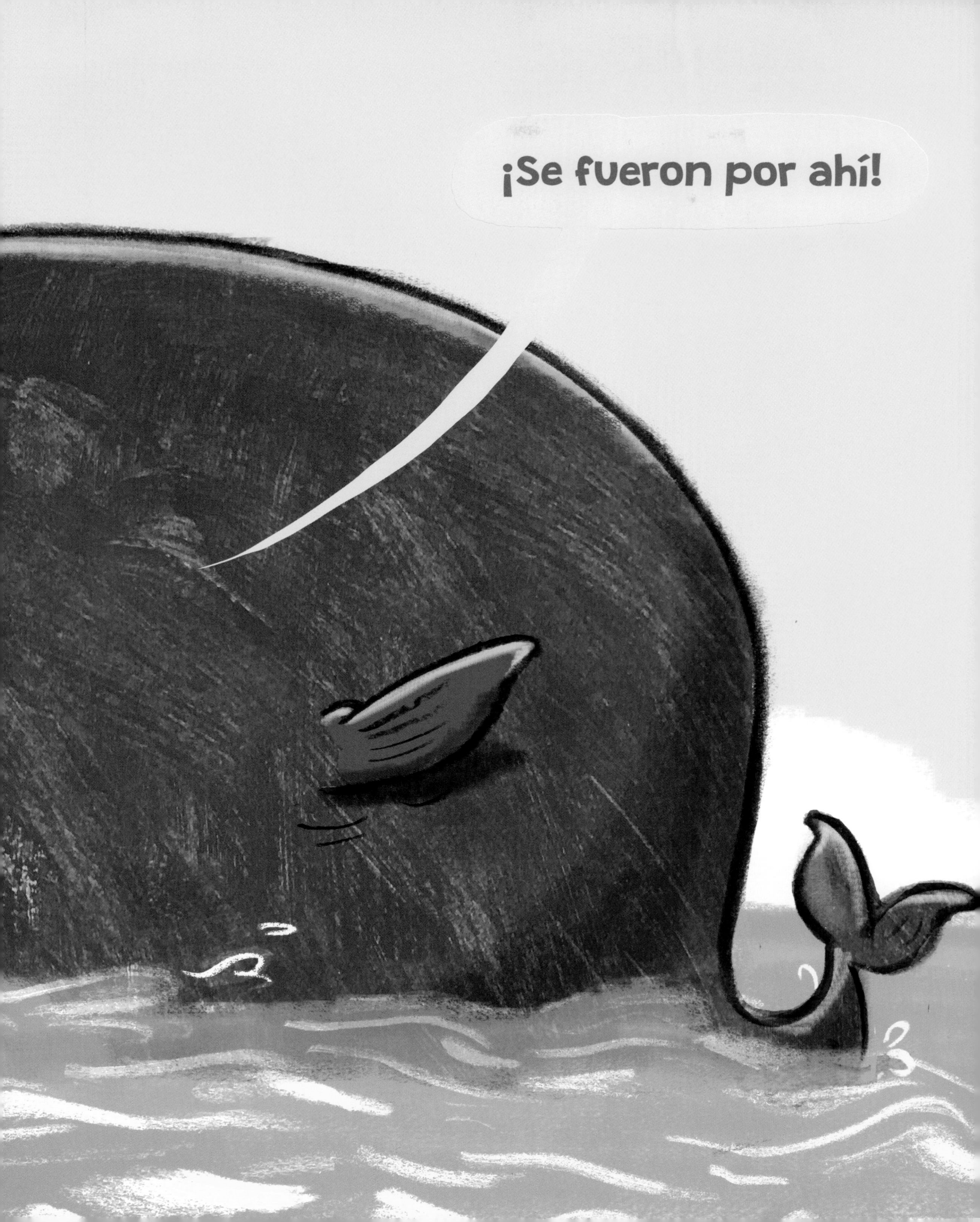
¡Se fueron por ahí!

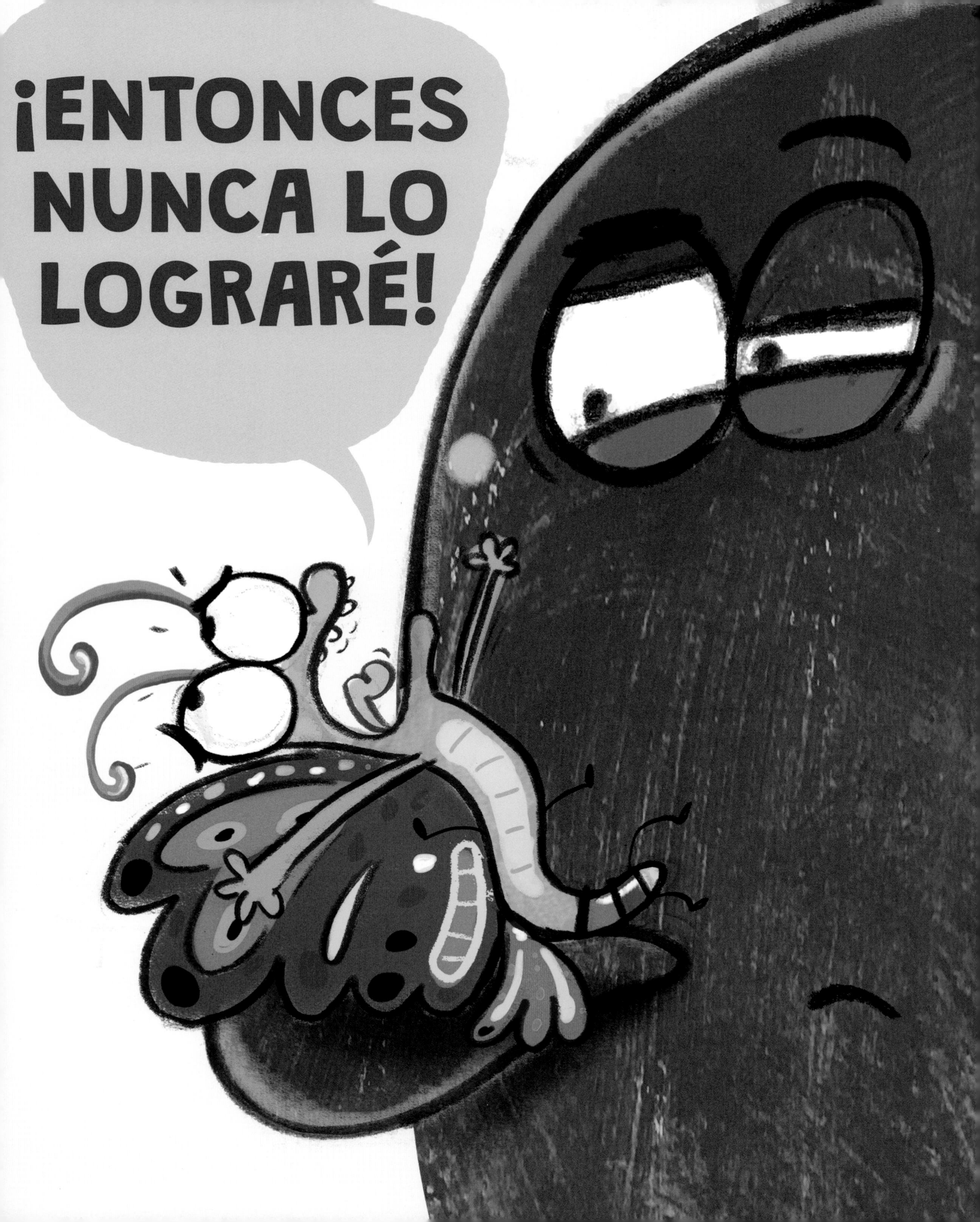
¡ENTONCES NUNCA LO LOGRARÉ!

La vida era mucho más simple cuando era una oruga.
¡Yo!
Construir la crisálida fue fácil.
Crisálida
(Estoy dentro).

Esperé pacientemente a convertirme en mariposa.

¡Tachán!

Entonces comenzó el viaje con los amigos en busca de flores.

Pero entonces...

las cosas se nublaron.

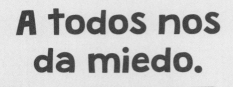

¿Hasta a ti?
Eres la criatura MÁS GRANDE del océano.
¡Pero el océano es MÁS GRANDE! A veces también siento mariposas en la panza.

Aquí hay MUCHO más espacio que en mi crisálida.
Kril
Hum... ¿No hay otra cosa que comer que no sea kril? ¿No? Pedire algo.
Hola... Un ramo de flores, por favor. Néctar extra. ¿La ocasión? Tengo hambre. ¿Dirección? Una ballena.
555 FLORES
— Clic —
¿Hola? ¿¿¿HOLAAA???

¡ESPERA! ¿No puedo vivir en tu panza PARA SIEMPRE?
No.
¿Qué te parece un contrato de un año?
¡No!
Tienes que seguir intentándolo.

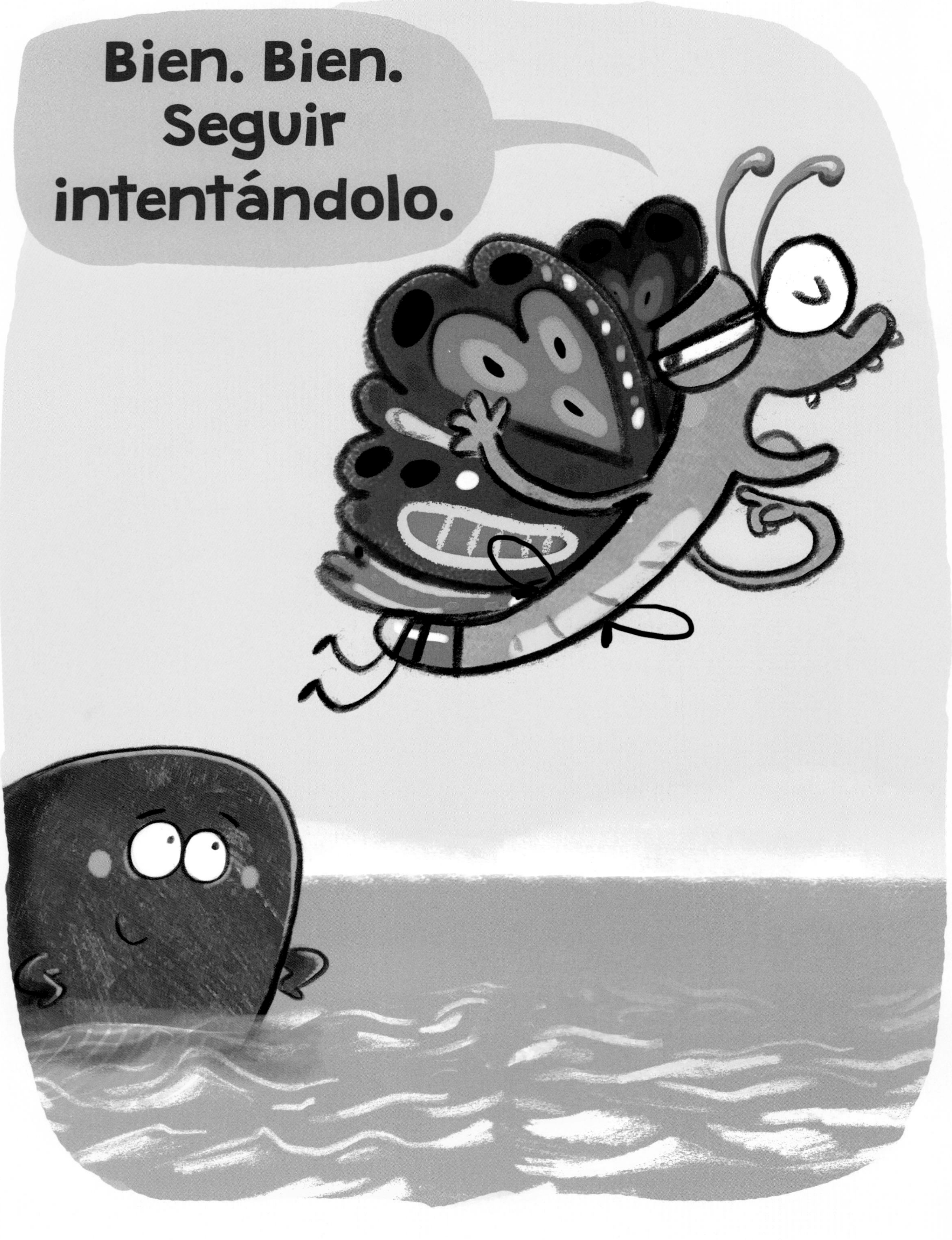
Bien. Bien. Seguir intentándolo.

¡No te rindas! SIGUE INTENTÁNDOLO.
ARRIBA MARIPOSA
Bien. Bien. SEGUIR INTENTÁNDOLO.
¡¡NADA podrá detenerme!!

Cree en
ti misma.

Bien... CREER en mí misma. ¡TÚ naciste para VOLAR!

¡Nací para LLORAR!

Lo ÚNICO que tienes que temer es...

¡TODO!

Si al principio no lo logras...

¡Deja de intentarlo!

NO. Si al principio no lo logras...

¡Vuela, vuela OTRA VEZ!

Mantén la dirección.

Kilómetro 40

El viento a favor.

Kilómetro 80

Que no te coman.

Kilómetro 160

Sigue intentándolo.

Kilómetro 200

Sigue volando.

Kilómetro 240

Sigue intentándolo.

320 kilómetros más tarde...

No hay NADA que no pueda lograr cuando creo en mí misma, ¿saben? ¡¡¡Podría volar UN MILLÓN DE KILÓMETROS MÁS!!!
¡Qué BUENO!
Ahora come antes de irnos a hibernar.

Para Lara, por ayudarme a encontrar mi camino en los libros ilustrados

Originally published in English as *The Little Butterfly That Could* · Translated by Abel Berriz · Copyright © 2021 by Ross Burach · Translation copyright © 2021 by Scholastic Inc. · All rights reserved. Published by Scholastic Inc., *Publishers Since 1920*. SCHOLASTIC, SCHOLASTIC EN ESPAÑOL, and associated logos are trademarks and/or registered trademarks of Scholastic Inc. The publisher does not have any control over and does not assume any responsibility for author or third-party websites or their content. · No part of this publication may be reproduced, stored in a retrieval system, or transmitted in any form or by any means, electronic, mechanical, photocopying, recording, or otherwise, without written permission of the publisher. For information regarding permission, write to Scholastic Inc., Attention: Permissions Department, 557 Broadway, New York, NY 10012. · This book is a work of fiction. Names, characters, places, and incidents are either the product of the author's imagination or are used fictitiously, and any resemblance to actual persons, living or dead, business establishments, events, or locales is entirely coincidental. · ISBN 978-1-338-74599-3 · 10 9 8 7 6 5 4 3 2   21 22 23 24 25 · Printed in U.S.A.   40 · First Spanish printing, 2021 · Ross Burach's art was created with pencil, crayon, acrylic paint, and digital coloring. · The text type was set in Grandstander Classic Bold. · The display type was set in Grandstander Classic Bold. · The book was art directed and designed by Marijka Kostiw. Original edition edited by Tracy Mack.